To my beautiful daughter Olivia.

Olivia and
the little red fox

Written and Illustrated
by Golnar Sepahi

Olivia lived in a small, cozy house at the edge of the woods with her mom and dad.

One winter morning she looked
out her bedroom window to find
snow had covered the ground.

Olivia loved the snow, so she
bundled into her coat, hat, scarf
and gloves. She kissed her mom
and dad and ran out the door.

"Wow!" she exclaimed. "It looks magical!"
Birds sang and squirrels jumped from branch to branch. Olivia even saw an owl sleeping on a perch.

She was just beginning to build
a snowman when she heard a cry.
It was coming from a nearby tree.

Unsure of what was making the noise,
Olivia tiptoed towards the tree,
to discover a little red fox hiding.

"Are you lost?" she asked the little red fox.
  He nodded.
"Want me to help you find your mother?"
  The little red fox nodded again,
  and off they went.

Luckily, the little red fox's paw prints were
clearly visible in the snow.
"All we need to do now is follow your tracks."
Olivia explained.

After walking for a short time the tracks led them
to a frozen lake. Olivia turned to the little red fox.
"Have you ever gone skating on ice before?"
she asked. He shook his head, no.

"It's fun!" she said. The little red fox followed
Olivia onto the ice. They began racing back
and forth going faster each time until finally,
they fell laughing on the far bank.

"Let's make snow angels," Olivia said.
She and the little red fox lay in the snow, looking
up at the sky, waving their arms up and down.

"Have you ever tasted snow?"
"No," the little red fox nodded.
"Try it." Olivia scooped some snow into a ball
and threw it up in the air. The little red fox
leaped up and caught it, eating it with a smile.

She and the red fox were having so much
fun they forgot to look for his mother.
Even worse, Olivia had to get back home.
"We need to hurry!" Olivia said. They began hunting
for any new sign of the little red fox's tracks.

They quickly followed the trail
and fortunately it did lead to
the little red fox's mother.

The little red fox was so happy
he ran to his mother arms.

By then the sun was setting
so the two foxes helped
Olivia return home safely.

At that moment Olivia realized that friends come in all shapes and sizes. From that day on she knew she had found a little friend in the woods.